# Nuri and the Whale

Green
Bean
Books

First published in 2021 by Agam Publishing House, Israel
First published in the UK in 2022 by Green Bean Books
c/o Pen & Sword Books Ltd
47 Church Street, Barnsley, South Yorkshire, S70 2AS
www.greenbeanbooks.com

Green Bean Books edition: 978-1-78438-806-5
Harold Grinspoon Foundation edition: 978-1-78438-810-2

Designed by Ian Hughes
Edited by Kate Baker, Julie Carpenter and Lisa Silverman
Production by Hugh Allan

Printed in China by Printworks Global Ltd, London and Hong Kong
1022/B1915/A7

FSC
www.fsc.org
100%
Paper from well-
managed forests
FSC® C152346

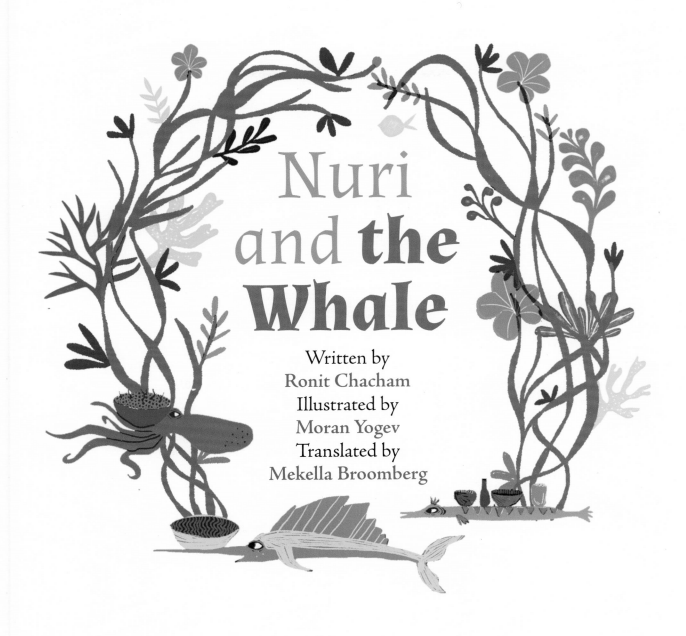

# Nuri and **the** **Whale**

Written by
Ronit Chacham
Illustrated by
Moran Yogev
Translated by
Mekella Broomberg

Green
Bean
Books

# CHAPTER I

A long time ago, there was a young man named Nuri
who loved to visit the sea.

When he reached the shore, he would eat some bread
and throw a piece into the waves.

He did this because his father once told him:
"Cast your bread on the water."

Nuri loved his father very much, so he followed his advice,
even though he didn't understand why he had to do it.

The small fish kept returning to enjoy Nuri's bread.
And he grew bigger and bigger.

Soon he was so big that he frightened the other fish, and
they complained to Wisewhale, the King of the Sea.

"There's one fish who eats and eats. He's growing so
enormous that soon he'll want to eat us too!"

Wisewhale asked to meet the small fish.

"How have you grown so large?"
Wisewhale asked.

The fish explained that Nuri threw
bread into the water every day and
Wisewhale asked to meet him too.

## CHAPTER II

The next day, the fish spotted Nuri
at the usual place.

He moved closer and waited.

At that moment, Nuri saw the fish near the shore.

He inched forward, but as he did, he slipped and fell into the water.

The fish opened his mouth and swallowed Nuri in one gulp!

Nuri sat in the belly of the fish and gazed through
his eyes, marveling at all the treasures hidden
beneath the ocean's waves.

When they finally reached the ocean's floor,
Nuri emerged from the fish's mouth and found
himself in the palace of the King of the Sea.
He was astonished by its beauty.

Who is this important young man?

What has he done?

Wisewhale treated Nuri as an honored guest and served him the finest delicacies that Nuri had ever tasted.

Wisewhale then asked, "Why do you throw food into the water every day?"

Nuri answered, "My father used to say, 'cast your bread on the water.'"

"But do you know the next part of that saying?"

Nuri shook his head. "I can't remember it!"

עַל פְּנֵי הַמַּיִם,

תִּמְצָאֵנוּ.

שְׁלַח לַחְמְךָ

כִּי בְרֹב הַיָּמִים

"Cast your bread on the water, and one day it will come back to you," Wisewhale explained.

"Yes, that's it exactly!" cried Nuri. "But wait. How is it that we can understand each other?"

Wisewhale replied, "When you stood staring at the beauty of my palace, I gave you all the languages spoken by the animals of the land and sea."

"But what will I do with so many languages?" asked Nuri.

"That," said Wisewhale, "is for you to discover."

"Thank you, King of the Sea, for all these amazing gifts," said Nuri.

"But one more thing," continued Wisewhale. "For the time being, don't throw any more bread into the sea!

"And know that there will be days to come when you will give and take – and you will be both happy and sad."

Nuri didn't understand what Wisewhale meant, but he promised to do as he was told.

Wisewhale then called to the big fish and asked him to carry Nuri back to dry land.

## CHAPTER III

Nuri returned home with a heavy heart. He had felt happy when he threw bread into the water – so what would he do now?

Many days passed. Then one night, as Nuri lay on his bed, unable to sleep, he saw two geckos on his windowsill.

They were talking to each other!

"Look at this man," said one gecko. "He leads such a simple life and has no idea what is hidden beneath him."

Nuri sat up. "I heard you!" he exclaimed.

"What? Do you speak Gecko?"
asked one gecko.

"It seems so," replied Nuri.

"So we can tell you that treasure is buried below
the bed here!"

Nuri dug under his bed, and the geckos were right! He found a box of gems!

Thank you, charming geckos!

Nuri sold the gems, and with the money he built the grandest house in the village.

## CHAPTER IV

Time passed. And then one day, when Nuri returned home from the market, he overheard his donkeys talking.

"Know that there will be days to come when you will give and take – and you will be both happy and sad."

"How did such a simple man manage to get all these riches?"

"They say he met the King of the Sea, who taught him something important."

"And it all happened because he fed a fish?"

"No. It all happened because he shared what little he had."

Nuri listened to the conversation of the donkeys;
then he finally knew what he needed to do.

Nuri set up a round table in his beautiful home. In the entrance, he put up a sign welcoming visitors and offering them food and drink.

The story of Nuri's generosity spread across the land.
People who passed by his village were invited to come
to his home to rest, wash the dust from their feet, and
eat their fill.

## EPILOGUE

In time, Nuri married. The house
filled with sons and daughters.

His children also had children, and
when he grew old, Nuri gathered his family
around him and said to them:

"Sometimes in life you'll have everything, and sometimes you'll have almost nothing. But give to others even if you have only a little. Those who open their hearts to others will be rewarded in the end."

"What will the reward be?" asked the children.

"Sometimes treasure, sometimes a smile, and sometimes a joyful heart."

And then Nuri told them the story you have just heard.

שַׁלַּח לַחְמְךָ עַל פְּנֵי הַמָּיִם,
כִּי בְרֹב הַיָּמִים תִּמְצָאֶנּוּ.

Cast your bread on the water,
and one day it will come back to you.
— *Kohelet 11:1*